Someone's Got a Screw Loose

Nancy Krulik and Amanda Burwasser

Someone's Got a Screw Loose

Illustrated by Mike Moran

Sky Pony Press
New York

First Edition

While this book aims to accurately describe the steps a child should able to perform
reasonably independently, a supervising adult should be present at all times. The authors,
illustrator, and publisher take no responsibility for any injury cause while making a project
from this book.

This is a work of fiction. Names, characters, places, and incidents are from the authors'
imaginations, and used fictitiously.

Sky Pony Press books may be purchased in bulk at special discounts for sales promotion,
corporate gifts, fund-raising, or educational purposes. Special editions can also be created to
specifications. For details, contact the Special Sales Department, Sky Pony Press, 307 West
36th Street, 11th Floor, New York, NY 10018 or info@skyhorsepublishing.com.

Sky Pony® is a registered trademark of Skyhorse Publishing, Inc.®, a Delaware corporation.

Visit our website at www.skyponypress.com.

www.realnancykrulik.com
www.mikemoran.net

10 9 8 7 6 5 4 3 2

Library of Congress Cataloging-in-Publication Data

Names: Krulik, Nancy E., author. | Burwasser, Amanda Elizabeth, author. |
Moran, Michael, 1957- illustrator.
Title: Someone's got a screw loose / Nancy Krulik and Amanda Burwasser ;
illustrated by Mike Moran.
Other titles: Someone has got a screw loose
Description: First edition. | New York : Skyhorse Publishing, [2018] |
Summary: An invitation to a birthday party becomes a recipe for disaster
when Java's secret is nearly exposed by a nosy reporter.
Identifiers: LCCN 2018006396 (print) | LCCN 2018014768 (ebook) | ISBN
9781510726697 (eb) | ISBN 9781510726642 (hardcover) | ISBN 9781510726697
(ebook)
Subjects: | CYAC: Robots--Fiction. | Birthdays--Fiction. | Parties--Fiction.
| Humorous stories.
Classification: LCC PZ7.K9416 (ebook) | LCC PZ7.K9416 Sok 2018 (print) | DDC
[Fic]--dc23
LC record available at https://lccn.loc.gov/2018006396

Cover illustration by Mike Moran
Cover design by Kate Gartner

Paperback ISBN: 978-1-5107-2656-7
Ebook ISBN: 978-1-5107-2669-7

Printed in the United States of America

For Alison Weiss, our supportive editor extraordinaire,

who never tells us we *can't* do it!

—AB & NK

To my Project Droid teammates, a big thank you!

—MM

CONTENTS

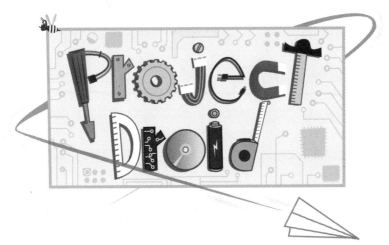

Someone's Got a Screw Loose

1.

You're Invited?

"Here."

Sherry Silverspoon shoved an envelope into my hand during recess Wednesday afternoon.

"Here."

Jerry Silverspoon shoved an envelope into my cousin Java's hand.

"What's this?" I asked the twins.

"It's an invitation to a birthday party," Java said. He had already opened his envelope and was reading the card inside.

"You're inviting us to your party?" I was surprised. The twins and I are not friends. *At all.* "Is this some sort of joke?"

"No joke. You're both invited," Sherry said. She did not sound happy about it.

"Our mom made us invite the whole third grade," Jerry explained.

Okay, now the invitation made sense.

"No one says you have to *come* to our party," Sherry said. "We won't be upset if you don't show up."

"Not as long as you get us presents," Jerry added.

"*Good* presents," Sherry insisted.

I looked at the invitation. The twins'
party was going to be a big carnival in
their yard. And since they had invited
our whole grade, lots of my friends
would be there.

"We wouldn't miss it," I said. "Would we, Java?"

Java thought for a minute. Then he said, "According to my internal calendar, I have the date free. I will come."

"Your *internal calendar*?" Jerry repeated.

"You better not talk all strange like that when you're at our party," Sherry warned. "You might get quoted in the newspaper."

What was she talking about?

"Why would your party be in the newspaper?" I asked them.

"This backyard carnival party is going to be a huge deal," Jerry explained. "Our parents have invited some very important people. Newspapers do articles about parties with important people."

"So don't act like loony tunes," Sherry added. "We don't want the whole town thinking we hang out with weirdos."

"What's that supposed to mean?" I demanded.

"According to the dictionary in my hard drive, a weirdo is a person who acts or dresses strangely," Java told me.

"*That's* what we mean." Jerry glared at us and walked away with Sherry to hand out more invitations.

weirdo (noun)
a person whose
dress or behavior

It wasn't going to be easy getting Java to act like a regular third-grade kid at that party.

That's because Java isn't a regular third-grade kid.

Java isn't a kid at all. He's an android.

My mom is a scientist. And Java is part of a secret experimental project she is working on: **Project Droid**.

The whole point of Project Droid is to figure out if an android can fit in with real people. So Java is programmed to do all sorts of real-kid things—like go to school or play soccer or try out for the school play.

Only he doesn't always do those things the same way a real kid would.

And he doesn't always understand what real kids are talking about.

"Listen, you can't talk about your hard drive or your internal calendar or any computer stuff at this party," I told Java.

"Why not?" Java asked me.

Well, for starters, I didn't want some snoopy reporter figuring out Java's secret. And for another . . .

"If you act strange at the Silverspoons' party, they're never going to let *me* forget it," I told my cousin. "We have to get through this party without causing any trouble. And we have to get the twins gifts they'll really like."

"What do you think they would like?" Java asked.

"I don't know yet," I admitted. "But I'll figure it out. I'm going to ask Mom to drive us to the mall after school."

"Your mother cannot drive us anywhere today," Java told me.

"Why not?" I asked.

"Because her car is in the shop," Java pointed out.

"Okay. Then you, Mom, and I can just grab a bus."

Java gave me a strange smile. He crossed his eyes. And wiggled his ears. Then he shouted, "**I can do it!**"

The next thing I knew, my cousin was running toward the school parking lot.

He raced over toward a long line of yellow school buses.

And then, with just one hand, he *grabbed*
a bus—and lifted it right off the ground!
Androids are really, really strong.

I raced over to the parking lot. My head was thumping. This was bad.

I was never going to be able to keep Java's true identity a secret now. If even one kid in the schoolyard saw what my cousin was doing . . .

But no one did. The kids were all too busy playing games, talking to each other, and wondering why the Silverspoon twins had invited them to their birthday party to notice Java.

"Put that down," I ordered my cousin when I caught up to him.

"You said we needed to grab a bus," Java reminded me.

I shook my head. Asking Java not to act like a weirdo was really asking a lot.

2.

Making a Scene

"You boys look around Toyz Be You," Mom told Java and me later that afternoon, at the mall. "I need to pick up a lug wrench at Schmoopies Hardware Store. I'll meet you here in a few minutes."

"We have to find really good gifts for Jerry and Sherry," I told Java as we

walked into the toy store. "Something they won't make fun of."

Java held up a package of socks with pictures of baseballs, footballs, and soccer balls all over them. "How about these?" he asked.

Java was really smart about a lot of things. He knew exactly how many miles it is from Toad Suck, Arkansas, to Chicken Bristle, Illinois.

He could tell you the total population of Kazakhstan right off the top of his head.

And he could figure out a math problem, like four thousand nine hundred sixty-seven divided by forty-three, without picking up a pencil.

But when it came to a great birthday present, he had absolutely no clue.

"Keep looking," I told him.

I scanned the shelves, searching for the perfect gift.

But nothing I saw seemed right.

Not the plumber action figure with its own electric plunger.

Or the pooper-scooper board game.

Or the box of golf balls that looked like eyeballs.

Getting the twins their birthday gifts was going to be hard.

"Maybe they would like something with a remote

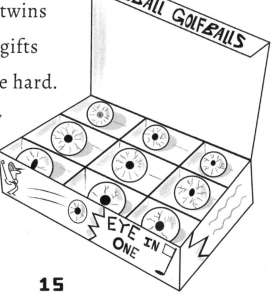

15

control," I murmured as I turned the corner. "Or a—"

SLAM!

CRASH!

BOUNCE. BOUNCE. BOUNCE.

I wasn't looking where I was going. I fell right into a giant display of rubber balls. *Which were now bouncing their way all over the store.*

"Logan, are you okay?"

I looked up to see my best friend, Stanley, standing over me.

"Yeah, I'm fine," I told him as I struggled to my feet.

A bunch of people in purple Toyz Be You T-shirts went racing by, scrambling to catch the runaway bouncing balls.

A few of them gave me dirty looks.

"Stupid Silverspoon twins," I
muttered. "This is all their fault."

"I guess you and Java are here to get gifts for Jerry and Sherry, too, huh?" Stanley asked.

Just then, Java came running toward us. He was dribbling one of the rubber balls with his hands.

Bounce. Bounce. Bounce-bounce-bounce-bounce.

"Wow!" Stanley exclaimed. "I never saw anyone dribble that fast."

"I cannot dribble," Java told Stanley. "I cannot drool

either. There is no spit in my body. My mechanisms are dry."

Stanley gave Java a funny look. "Huh?"

"Java just means he's really, really thirsty," I said quickly. "You know. Like he's got a dry mouth."

"Oh." Stanley laughed. "You're funny, Java."

"Dribbling is what basketball players call it when they bounce a ball," I explained to my cousin.

A weird whirring sound came from Java's belly. I'm pretty sure he was inputting the information into his hard drive.

"I was surprised when Sherry and Jerry gave me the invitation," I told Stanley, changing the subject.

"Me, too," Stanley agreed. "I think everyone was." Then he added, "Don't turn around."

"Why not?" I asked.

"*She's* here," Stanley answered.

I didn't have to ask who *she* was. I knew Stanley meant Nadine Vardez.

My palms began to sweat.

My fingers began to twitch.

And the little hairs on my arms all stood up.

Why do I always get so nervous around Nadine?

"Hi, you guys," Nadine said as she walked over.

"Olleh," I mumbled.

Nadine gave me a strange look.

I didn't blame her. I was so shaky, I was talking backward.

"Are you here to get presents for the twins, too?" Stanley asked Nadine.

She nodded. "But I haven't found anything yet."

"We haven't either," Stanley said.

"I guess we're just gonna have to keep looking," Nadine said. "I'm going over to the sporting goods section. See you later."

As Nadine walked away, I shook my head. "'Olleh?'" I groaned. "That was really dumb."

Stanley didn't argue with me.

"I don't know what it is with me," I continued. "Every time Nadine comes by, I feel all weird. My stomach gets jumpy and it's like fireworks go off in my head."

Java shot me a crooked a smile. His
nose twitched. His eyes rolled around in
his head.

"I can do it!" he shouted.

POP! POP! POP! Suddenly, loud noises
started coming out of Java's mouth.
Bright colored lasers shot from his eyes.
Then he burst up in the air and
whirled around in a circle.

It was like he was a giant android fireworks show.

But androids don't turn to smoke and disappear in midair the way fireworks do.

Androids come down to earth. *With a THUD.*

My android cousin landed right in the middle of a big pile of space alien action figures.

The space aliens went flying through the air, like . . . well . . . *space aliens.*

Stanley stared at Java. "How did—?" he began.

Before I could come up with a good answer, a group of people in Toyz Be You shirts came running over again.

"That's it!" one of them shouted at us.
"First the bouncing balls, and now the
aliens. You three have caused enough
trouble. GET OUT!"

3.

Read My Lips

"How do you wrap an elephant's trunk?" I wondered out loud.

It was Saturday morning. The twins' party was in a few hours. Java and I were wrapping their gifts.

Mom had picked up matching stuffed elephants for Jerry and Sherry. I didn't know why. But stuffed elephants were what we had, so stuffed elephants were what we were giving them.

"Directions for wrapping elephants is not in my hard drive," Java told me. "But I do have an elephant joke. What time is it when an elephant sits on your fence?"

"I don't know," I said.

"Time to get a new fence," Java said. "Isn't that a funny joke, Logan?"

"Sure," I said. I didn't want to hurt his feelings—although I'm never really sure if Java *has* feelings. "Let's just finish wrapping these things. I still have to get dressed."

"You are dressed," Java said. "You are wearing pants and a shirt."

"I can't wear this to a party!" I explained, horrified. "I have to wear party clothes."

Java looked at me blankly. He didn't understand. But why would he?

Java didn't care what he looked like. Robots never do.

But *I* cared.

"What do you think of this?" I asked as I put on a pair of blue-and-white-checked pants and my green-and-yellow-striped shirt.

Java shook his head. "I am not programmed to know what is fashionable," he told me.

I guess I wasn't either. Looking in the mirror at the stripes and checks was making me dizzy.

I pulled out my new tan slacks and my red button-down shirt, which looked great, until I saw the shirt had two buttons missing.

I guessed I could put on the cowboy shirt my cousin had sent me from Montana three years ago. It was pretty cool, and I had never had the chance to wear it.

And I never would. Because now it was *way* too small.

"I guess I'm just going to have to wear my regular school clothes," I said, pulling on a pair of jeans with big pockets and a long-sleeved shirt. "I sure hope this isn't a dressy party."

"Are carnivals dressy?" Java asked me.

"Not usually," I told him. "But this is the *Silverspoons'* carnival. And they don't do things like other people do."

"Is that bad?" Java wondered.

I didn't know how to answer that question. Java didn't do things like other people did either.

And some of the things Java did *were* pretty cool. And funny.

"Being different isn't always bad," I said. "But today, you have to try really hard to act like a real kid like everybody else."

"I am programmed to act like a real kid," Java insisted.

That was not something a real kid would say.

"Java," I told him, "read my lips. Today you have to ACT NORMAL."

Java moved his eyes up and down. He cocked his head to the side. Then he shouted out, "**I can do it!**"

Java yanked my jaw open and peered into my mouth.

"Wha-sha doin'?" I mumbled.

"Reading your lips," he said. "Or trying to. There are no words printed there."

Oh, brother. If Java was looking for something to read, he probably should have tried the calendar instead.

Because this day had *doom* written all over it.

4

Fancy-Schmancy

"Now remember," I told Java later that afternoon as we walked up the steps to the Silverspoons' giant front porch, "no funny stuff."

"I can't tell jokes?" Java said. "Because there's a new one in my data file. It's about firefighters and red suspenders."

"No jokes," I told him.

I felt kind of bad. I didn't want to tell Java not to be himself. That wasn't nice. Still, it was just for today.

I ran my hand through my hair. Slimy gel oozed all over my fingers.

I had tried to give myself a cool new hairstyle for the party. Maybe I had overdone it, though. When I rang the doorbell, my fingers left a greasy hair gel stain by the door.

The Silverspoons' doorbell didn't go *ding-dong* like a normal bell. Instead, it played a whole song.

"That's fancy-schmancy," I told Java.

"I do not think *schmancy* is a word," Java replied. "It is not anywhere in my dictionary.

"Hello, Logan," Mrs. Silverspoon said when she answered the door. "That's quite an interesting hairstyle you have there. And who is this?"

"My cousin, Java," I said. "He just came to live with us a few months ago."

"I was Sherry and Jerry's partner at the science fair," Java reminded her. "We studied bees."

"Oh yes." Mrs. Silverspoon nodded. "I remember now."

It would be hard to forget something like that. All the bees in Java's science project had gotten loose. Everyone in the gym had gotten stung.

"Thank you for inviting us to the party," Java said.

I rolled my eyes. I knew he was just saying that because my mom had programmed him to be polite.

But Mrs. Silverspoon didn't know that. She smiled at Java and said, "You are adorable."

Java smiled back and shouted, "**I can do it!**" Then he began to sing the same song the Silverspoons' doorbell played. *Loudly.*

Mrs. Silverspoon jumped back, surprised.

"She said 'adorable,'" I whispered. "Not a doorbell."

"Oh," Java said. "I am sorry. My language recognition software must have a glitch."

Mrs. Silverspoon gave Java a funny look and shook her head.

"The carnival is in the backyard," she finally told us. "Why don't you leave your gifts on the table, and then head out there?"

"Okay," I replied. Java and I placed our stuffed elephants on the gift table. There were lots of presents there already. A whole mountain of them. I wondered if the other gifts were better than our stuffed elephants.

But there wasn't time to think about that now. Mrs. Silverspoon was staring at Java like he had three heads.

She had definitely noticed there was something *different* about him.

And besides, there was a carnival waiting for us.

"Come on!" I said, pulling Java by the arm. "Let's go have some fun!"

"Do you believe this party?" Stanley asked us a few minutes later when we met up with him near the baseball-throwing booth.

"It's amazing," I agreed.

This was no ordinary backyard carnival. The Silverspoons had made their whole yard look like the real deal.

There were games to play and prizes to win.

There was a bouncy castle and a giant slide.

There was also a photo booth, a popcorn stand, a hot dog grill, and a cotton candy machine.

Everyone seemed to be having a really good time.

Maybe because no one seemed to be hanging around with Jerry and Sherry.

"Have you seen the twins yet?" I asked Stanley.

He shook his head. "We should say hello. But I don't know how we could find them. There are so many people."

"Sherry and Jerry are by the trees," Java said, pointing. "They are talking with the woman in the red dress."

"You spotted them all the way over there?" Stanley asked. He sounded really impressed. "You have an eagle eye!"

"Actually, an eagle can see more than three miles away," Java told him. "I am only programmed to see two miles away."

"Stanley didn't mean a real eagle—" I started to explain.

But Stanley interrupted me. "I didn't

know you were into birds," he told Java, sounding really excited. "I love bird-watching! Last week I saw a rare pink-footed goose! We should go together sometime."

Phew. Saved by the bird.

I didn't want to give Java another chance to spout off any more weird, random facts, so I pointed to the baseball-throwing game.

"Anyone want to try and win a giant stuffed pineapple?" I asked.

5.

Plush Pineapples and Fluffy Fish

Clink. Clunk. Clonk.

I watched as the top three cups from the pyramid fell onto the table below.

Stanley frowned. He'd thrown that baseball at the cups as hard as he could.

"Not bad," the guy behind the baseball-throwing booth told him.

"Knocking down three cups is better than none."

"It's not good enough to win the giant stuffed pineapple, though," Stanley said. "It's not even good enough to win the little stuffed fish in the corner. And that one's missing a fin."

"No one ever wins at these games," I told Stanley.

"I know," he agreed. "Maybe—"

CRASH!

Before Stanley could finish his sentence, I heard a loud noise.

The ground shook.

It felt like an earthquake.

Only it wasn't. It was a *Java*-quake! And it left my cousin standing in a pile of stuffed fish, leopards, and pineapples.

A crowd of people hurried over.

"I don't believe that kid!" the guy running the booth said. "He didn't just knock over the cups. He knocked over *everything!*"

Java stepped out from the pile of prizes. He handed Stanley a giant stuffed pineapple. "This is for you," Java said. Then he reached into his pocket and pulled out a tiny stuffed fish. "And this, too."

"Thanks," Stanley said, amazed. "How did you do that?"

"I threw the ball," Java answered simply.

Just then, I spotted a woman in a red dress hurrying over to the baseball booth. She was the same woman who had been talking to Jerry and Sherry before.

Only now she wasn't talking. She was writing in a notebook.

She had to be the newspaper reporter. Which meant the less she saw of Java, the better.

"When Jerry and Sherry see this, they're going to be really mad," I told Stanley and Java. "Let's get out of here."

"You're right," Stanley agreed.

"How about we go to the photo booth?" I suggested. "That's always fun."

"Great," Stanley said, "but first I gotta go to the porta potty. I drank too much lemonade."

"We'll meet you by the photo booth," I told him.

As my cousin and I walked across the yard, I shook my head. "I can't believe you knocked down the whole game tent," I said.

"Did I do something wrong?" Java asked me.

I didn't know how to answer that. Java really hadn't done anything wrong. It wasn't his fault he was super strong.

"I guess not," I told him as we neared the photo booth. "Look at this line. By the time we get our pictures taken, the party will be over."

Java smiled. "I can take your picture, Logan. Say 'aged gouda.'"

I looked at him strangely. "Say *what*?"

"You know, say 'cheese,'" Java replied.

He blinked twice.

And sneezed once.

Then he opened his mouth.

A piece of paper rolled out over his tongue.

"Here are your photos, Logan," Java said as he handed me the paper.

Sure enough, they were pictures of me. *Lousy* pictures of me. My mouth was all twisted, one of my eyes was closed, and my hair was standing straight up.

"Your mother updated my systems last week," Java told me. "I can do many new things. Would you like me to—"

"NO!" I shouted, stopping Java mid-sentence. "How about you wait here for Stanley? I'm going to get some popcorn. Then I'll be right back."

"Okay, Logan," Java agreed.

I had barely taken a few steps when I stopped in my tracks.

There was that reporter again. She was hiding behind some bushes.

But I could still tell she was staring at

Java. And writing in her notebook. I had
a bad feeling she'd seen everything.

Suddenly, I wasn't hungry anymore.

6.

Sneaky Snoop

"Java! We have to go home . . . *now!*" I shouted as I raced back toward the photo booth.

But Java wasn't there.

He'd disappeared.

How was that possible? I'd only turned my back on him for a minute.

But that was all it took.

I had to find Java—and fast. There was no telling what kind of trouble he could get into.

But there were so many kids at the party. And the yard was huge. How was I going to find him?

"Go, Java! Go, Java!"

Just then, I heard a crowd of kids chanting my cousin's name.

"Go, Java! Go, Java!"

I followed the sounds of their voices.

I reached the high striker game just in time to see Java picking up the giant hammer.

Nadine and Stanley were standing by his side, cheering.

Uh-oh. Java didn't know his own strength. He could do some serious damage at a game like this.

"Java! No!" I shouted.

BAM!

Too late.

Java had already slammed the hammer down onto the lever.

The metal puck flew up.

CLANG! The puck hit the bell.

But instead of coming back down, the puck kept on flying—straight off the high striker and into the air.

I stood there, waiting for the puck to fall back down to earth.

But it never did. For all I knew, the puck had landed on the moon.

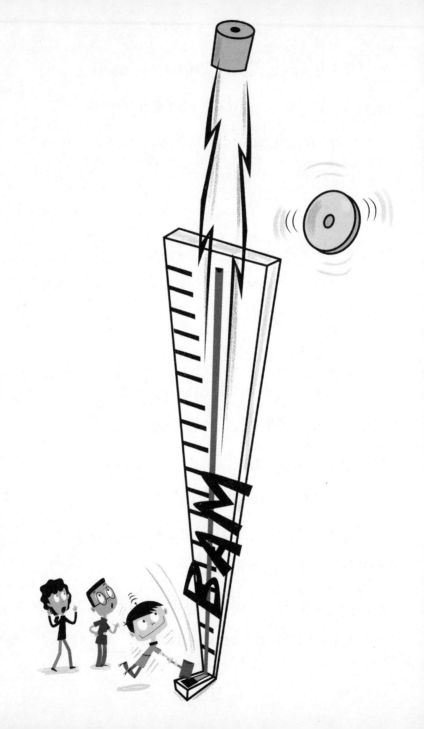

It could have happened. Java's *really* strong.

"Amazing!" Stanley gasped.

"Hooray for Java!" Nadine cheered like Java was a superhero or something.

Which he is not.

He's just an android.

And he's only that strong because my mom programmed him that way.

Click. Click. Click.

Just then, I heard someone's camera phone clicking above me.

I looked up in the trees.

There was the reporter. She was perched on a branch, taking lots of pictures of Java.

What a sneaky snoop.

This was awful. If the reporter wrote her article all about Java instead of the party, the Silverspoon twins were going to be *really* mad.

But that wasn't what I worried me most.

I was worried about what would happen to Java if the reporter figured out his secret.

It was up to me to do something to stop her.

7.

It's All Up In the Air

"We've been looking everywhere for you, Logan!"

"Where's that monster of a cousin of yours?"

I was trying to make my way through the crowd to Java so I could take him home, when I was stopped by Jerry and Sherry. They looked like they were about to burst with anger.

"He's ruining our whole party," Jerry complained. He balled his hands into little fists and started jumping up and down.

"No one is paying any attention to *us*." Sherry whined, pounding her feet into the ground.

"I *was* really, really trying to find him and get him out of here," I told the twins, "but now I'm wasting time talking to you."

"I don't care how you do it," Sherry insisted. "Just get that freak-o geek-o out of here."

That was easier said than done.

Java had moved on to who knows where.

Timbuktu for all I knew.

"There he is!" Sherry pointed at the bouncy castle.

"Flopping around like a smelly old fish," Jerry added.

Suddenly, I heard a giant *POP!*

The roof of the bouncy castle burst

open, and my robot cousin shot right through it.

"How'd he do that?" I heard someone ask.

I groaned and raced over to the bouncy castle.

"It's time to go," I said as I grabbed Java by his ankle and pulled him out of the air and back down to earth.

"But I haven't had the chance to try the birthday cake yet," Java insisted. "According to my hard drive, *normal* kids eat cake at birthday parties."

"You don't eat cake," I whispered to him. "You don't eat *anything*."

I didn't want to be around when the twins made their birthday wish, anyway. I knew they'd wish Java and I would get lost.

"You can't leave now." The woman in the red dress jumped in front of us and blocked our path. "I have a few questions for you. My name is Jackie Pepperoni. I'm a reporter for the *Weekly Words* newspaper."

Uh-oh.

"I've noticed that there's something peculiar about you," she said, turning to face my cousin.

"Peculiar?" I started nervously laughing. "He's not peculiar. He's as average as a peanut butter sandwich."

"Are you kidding?" Jackie Pepperoni asked me. "I've never seen anyone jump as high as he can or throw a ball as hard. Where are you from, young man?"

"Logan's garage," Java answered.

"He just means we built him a room in our garage," I explained quickly.

"How do you explain him spitting those pictures out of his mouth?" Jackie Pepperoni demanded.

"You didn't see what you thought you saw," I told her. "It was all in your head."

"That's funny," Java said. "All I have in *my* head are wires and nuts and bolts."

Jackie Pepperoni started writing in her reporter's notebook again.

I slapped the notebook out of her hand. I couldn't let her write about Java. It would ruin everything!

"My notes!" she shouted. "You knocked them into the punch bowl. They're ruined. But don't worry. It won't stop me from writing about the incredible things your cousin can do."

"Sometimes you can't believe your eyes," I insisted. "Those were just tricks. *Magic* tricks. I'm a great magician."

"Oh yeah?" Jackie Pepperoni replied. *"Prove it."*

8

Abraca-oops!

"Ladies and gentlemen. Boys and girls!" I shouted. "It's time to be amazed by the mystery of magic!"

A group of kids was gathering around me near one of the picnic tables.

I tried not to look at the Silverspoons' faces. I was sure they hadn't planned on having a magic show in the middle of their birthday party.

Especially one starring me.

I knew they would hate my guts, but I had to do this. I had to keep Java's secret safe.

It was a good thing I never went anywhere without a few magic tricks up my sleeve—and in my pockets.

I yanked the back pocket of my jeans open and walked around the crowd. "Nothing in here," I assured them. "Or is there?"

I reached into my back pocket again, and this time I pulled out a blue scarf.

And a pink scarf.

And a yellow scarf.

And a green scarf.

And . . . my *underpants!*

Oh brother. That wasn't supposed to happen. How embarrassing.

A few kids clapped.

A lot of kids started to walk away.

And Jackie Pepperoni started taking notes on a napkin.

This wasn't going well. If I didn't do something soon, I would never be able to convince her that she hadn't seen Java do all those crazy things.

There was only one person who could help me do the ultimate magic trick.

"Will my magic assistant, Java Applebaum, please join me," I called into the crowd.

Java made his way through all of the kids who had actually stuck around and joined me by the table. "Here I am, Logan," he said. "What does a magic assistant do?"

A couple of kids started to giggle.

"Please lie down on the picnic table," I said, ignoring them.

Java did as he was told.

"I am going to cut my assistant in half, using nothing more that this plastic knife," I announced.

Now I had Jackie Pepperoni's attention! And everyone else's, too.

I started pretending to saw Java's legs off with a plastic knife that had been left on the picnic table. But really, I was unscrewing his legs from his body with my other hand.

Then I said the magic word, "*Abracadoopadoop!*"

The crowd gasped, as Java's legless body sat up tall.

Everyone started applauding like crazy. Even Jackie Pepperoni!

"And now, I will put my assistant back together!" I announced as I pushed Java back down and quickly screwed his legs back in place.

I said the magic word. *"Abraca-poodapood!"*

Java leaped off the table and landed on his own two feet.

Unfortunately, I'd put his legs on backward.

"I think I have a screw loose!" Java said.

Uh-oh, I thought. This could be bad.

But the audience was laughing. And cheering.

They thought this was all part of the
show.

And so I let them think that!

Jackie Pepperoni crumpled up her
note-covered napkin and threw it in the
trash. I guess she wasn't going to write
an article about Java after all.

I'd made the whole story disappear.
Just like a real magician.

9

Gourmet Sponges

"What do you think you're doing?" Sherry demanded as she ran up to me after the magic show.

"We never asked you to do magic tricks at *our* party," Jerry added. He looked furious.

"The magic show was abrac-amazing!" Jackie Pepperoni exclaimed. "I've changed my mind. Now I want to do my article about *you*, Logan."

Sherry's eyes flew open wide.

Jerry's jaw dropped. A fly flew in and landed on his tongue.

"You want to do a story about *him*?" Sherry gulped.

"And not *us*?" Jerry gasped.

Jackie Pepperoni nodded. "How did you do that last trick?" she asked me.

"He just unscrew—" Java began.

I shoved my hand over my cousin's mouth.

"A magician never reveals his secrets," I told Jackie Pepperoni.

"You don't want to do an article about them," Jerry insisted.

"It's *our* party after all," Sherry added. "And, besides, we're not weirdos like those two!"

"We're not weirdos," I shot back.

"What do *you* call someone who talks to refrigerators and electric mixers?" Sherry asked.

"Or who scores soccer goals with his butt?" Jerry added.

"Or saws wood with his teeth?" the twins said together.

I couldn't really argue with them. Those were pretty weirdo things to do.

And Java had done them all.

Arf! Arf!

Just then, I heard a loud racket coming from a nearby picnic table. I turned around just in time to see . . .

CRASH!

SPLAT!

"Pookie, no!" I heard Mrs. Silverspoon shout out.

The twins' poodle,

Pookie, had gotten loose in the yard and knocked over the giant birthday cake that had just been brought out. There was frosting all over everyone.

Now Pookie was happily jumping up and down and licking frosting from all the guests' faces.

"Oh no!" Sherry exclaimed.

"Not our ten-layer sponge cake with rhubarb frosting," Jerry shouted.

"It was *very* expensive!" Sherry told Jackie Pepperoni. "My father had it flown here from a bakery in Paris."

"And now our gourmet sponge cake is ruined," Jerry said.

Java smiled. He wiggled his ears. He scratched his behind. And then he shouted, "**I can do it!**"

Java raced over to the sponge-toss booth. He grabbed ten sponges and piled them up. Then he picked up one of the birthday candles that had toppled from the cake and stuck it on the top sponge.

"Here," he told Jerry and Sherry.

"There's no frosting, but plenty of sponges."

Jackie Pepperoni started to laugh.

"You're very funny," she told my cousin.

Jerry and Sherry stared at Java.

Then they stared at me.

And, for just a moment, I thought they were about to cry.

10.

Extra! Extra!

It was the party of the year!
Jerry and Sherry Silverspoon
turned ten at their backyard
carnival. The highlight of
the party was the fabulous
magician Logan Applebaum
and his assistant, Java.

"This is worse than I thought," Sherry said as I read Jackie Pepperoni's newspaper article aloud on the school bus.

"She hardly even mentioned us," Jerry added.

"Sure she did," Stanley said, reading over my shoulder. "It says right here:

> "I don't know why Jerry and Sherry invited me," Nadine Vardez, one of the Silverspoons' classmates said, "but I am sure glad they did. That was the best magic show I've ever seen."

"It wasn't that great," Jerry argued.

"It stunk worse than Logan's dirty sneakers," Sherry complained.

I ignored them and went back to reading the article out loud.

The lucky twins received 137 huge stuffed purple elephants as gifts from their guests.

"You guys got them stuffed elephants, too?" Stanley asked me.

I shrugged. "My mom picked them out."

"Mine, too," Stanley said. "There must have been a big sale on purple elephants."

"Did you know an elephant's trunk can weigh four hundred pounds?" Java blurted out suddenly.

Everyone on the bus stared at him.

"And did you know that elephants are so handy with their trunks, they can use them to pick up a grain of rice?" Java continued.

"Java's such a weirdo," Jerry said.

"He's the *king* of the weirdos," Sherry agreed.

"I think you're a really smart cookie," Nadine told Java.

Java smiled. He wiggled his ears. And then he shouted, "**I can do it!**"

The next thing I knew, Java had grabbed my lunch box. He opened the lid and pulled out one of my chocolate sandwich cookies.

Java twisted the cookie open and stared at the filling.

"This is not a smart cookie," he said. "There's no hard drive inside. Only a creamy filling."

Everyone on the bus started laughing.

Everyone except for Jerry and Sherry, that is. They just rolled their eyes and gave Java and me dirty looks.

But I really didn't care. For some reason, the way Sherry and Jerry felt about my cousin and me just didn't seem to matter anymore.

Java was smart.

And funny.

And a lot of fun to have around.

I actually felt lucky to have him as my cousin.

And that's not weird at all.

A Really Cool Magic Trick

You don't need an android assistant to amaze your friends with your magic skills. Everything you need to be a master magician can be found right in your own kitchen.

Your friends are guaranteed to be astounded when you lift an ice cube out of a glass using nothing more than a piece of string.

Or at least that what it will look like to them.

They don't know the magician's secret. But you do.

Here's what you'll need:

- ⚙ 1 full glass of water
- ⚙ 1 ice cube
- ⚙ 1 piece of string
- ⚙ A salt shaker

 1 full glass of water

 1 ice cube

 1 piece of string

 A salt shaker

Here's What You Do:

This trick has to be set up ahead of time.

1 About a minute before your magic show, place the ice cube in the full glass of water.

2 Lay the string over your ice cube.

3 Pour a dash of salt on top of the string. (Make sure no one in your audience sees you doing this.)

4

Ask your audience to take their seats. Hold up the glass of water and tell them, "I am going to lift this ice cube right out of the water, using nothing more than this piece of magic string." Of course everyone will be amazed. You can't lift ice from a glass with string.

5

Say the magic word:

"AbracaDroid!"

6 Gently pull the edge of the string out of the glass. The ice cube will remain attached to the string.

7 Take your bow as your audience cheers wildly at your amazing magic skills. They will have no idea how you performed such an extraordinary feat.

Here's the secret:

Salt makes ice melt more quickly by lowering its freezing temperature. (That's why people put salt over icy roads during the winter.) But when the salt melts from the ice cube into the water, the ice freezes up again. And since the string is on top of the ice, it becomes frozen onto the cube when the ice refreezes.

Remember, don't tell anyone why the trick works. A magician never reveals his secrets!

About the Authors

Nancy Krulik is the author of more than two hundred books for children and young adults including three *New York Times* bestsellers and the popular Katie Kazoo, Switcheroo; George Brown, Class Clown; and Magic Bone series. She lives in New York City with her husband and a crazy beagle mix. Visit her online at www.realnancykrulik.com.

Amanda Burwasser holds a BFA with honors in creative writing from Pratt Institute in New York City. Her senior thesis earned the coveted Pratt Circle Award. A preschool teacher, she resides in Forestville, California.

About the Illustrator

Mike Moran is a dad, husband, and illustrator. His illustrations can be seen in children's books, animation, magazines, games, World Series programs, and more. He lives in Florham Park, New Jersey. Visit him online at www.mikemoran.net.